Put Beginning Readers on the Right Track with ALL ABOARD READING™

The All Aboard Reading series is especially designed for beginning readers. Written by noted authors and illustrated in full color, these are books that children really want to read—books to excite their imagination, expand their interests, make them laugh, and support their feelings. With fiction and nonfiction stories that are high interest and curriculum-related, All Aboard Reading books offer something for every young reader. And with four different reading levels, the All Aboard Reading series lets you choose which books are most appropriate for your children and their growing abilities.

Picture Readers
Picture Readers have super-simple texts, with many nouns appearing as rebus pictures. At the end of each book are 24 flash cards—on one side is a rebus picture; on the other side is the written-out word.

Station Stop 1
Station Stop 1 books are best for children who have just begun to read. Simple words and big type make these early reading experiences more comfortable. Picture clues help children to figure out the words on the page. Lots of repetition throughout the text helps children to predict the next word or phrase—an essential step in developing word recognition.

Station Stop 2
Station Stop 2 books are written specifically for children who are reading with help. Short sentences make it easier for early readers to understand what they are reading. Simple plots and simple dialogue help children with reading comprehension.

Station Stop 3
Station Stop 3 books are perfect for children who are reading alone. With longer text and harder words, these books appeal to children who have mastered basic reading skills. More complex stories captivate children who are ready for more challenging books.

In addition to All Aboard Reading books, look for All Aboard Math Readers™ (fiction stories that teach math concepts children are learning in school); All Aboard Science Readers™ (nonfiction books that explore the most fascinating science topics in age-appropriate language); All Aboard Poetry Readers™ (funny, rhyming poems for readers of all levels); and All Aboard Mystery Readers™ (puzzling tales where children piece together evidence with the characters).

All Aboard for happy reading!

GROSSET & DUNLAP
Published by the Penguin Group
Penguin Group (USA) Inc., 375 Hudson Street, New York, New York 10014, USA
Penguin Group (Canada), 90 Eglinton Avenue East, Suite 700,
Toronto, Ontario M4P 2Y3, Canada
(a division of Pearson Penguin Canada Inc.)
Penguin Books Ltd., 80 Strand, London WC2R 0RL, England
Penguin Group Ireland, 25 St. Stephen's Green, Dublin 2, Ireland
(a division of Penguin Books Ltd.)
Penguin Group (Australia), 250 Camberwell Road,
Camberwell, Victoria 3124, Australia
(a division of Pearson Australia Group Pty. Ltd.)
Penguin Books India Pvt. Ltd., 11 Community Centre, Panchsheel Park,
New Delhi—110 017, India
Penguin Group (NZ), 67 Apollo Drive, Rosedale, North Shore 0632, New Zealand
(a division of Pearson New Zealand Ltd.)
Penguin Books (South Africa) (Pty.) Ltd., 24 Sturdee Avenue,
Rosebank, Johannesburg 2196, South Africa

Penguin Books Ltd., Registered Offices:
80 Strand, London WC2R 0RL, England

Library of Congress Control Number: 2009009296

ISBN 978-0-448-45252-4   10 9 8 7 6 5 4 3 2 1

All Aboard Reading™

Station Stop 1

(handwritten inscription) To Kaylee — Love, Grandma Yola + Pop Pops x 12-27-09

We Love You, Strawberry Shortcake!

By Sierra Harimann
Illustrated by Marci Beighley

Grosset & Dunlap
An Imprint of Penguin Group (USA) Inc.

Strawberry Shortcake
is a berry sweet girl.

She likes to show
her friends how much
she cares about them.

Strawberry's friends like
to show they care, too.

Plum Pudding has an idea.
Everyone can give
Strawberry a gift.

Raspberry Torte wants to throw
Strawberry a surprise party.

Both ideas are good.
The girls will have a party
<u>and</u> bring gifts!

Plum and Raspberry
know what to give Strawberry.
So do Lemon Meringue
and Blueberry Muffin.

Orange Blossom does not
know what to give Strawberry.
But then she gets an idea!

Strawberry's friends set up for the party. It will be berry fun!

It is almost party time.
Blueberry calls Strawberry.

She asks Strawberry
to come to the bookstore.
Strawberry says she will
come right away.

Strawberry opens the door.
What a surprise!

Lemon pours lemonade.
Raspberry serves fruit salad.

Plum is the first to give
Strawberry a gift.

It is a dance lesson!

Next, Blueberry
gives her gift
to Strawberry.

It is a book for
Strawberry's recipes.

Then, Lemon gives
her gift to Strawberry.
It is a haircut.

Next, Strawberry opens
a box from Raspberry.
Inside is a pretty,
new dress!

Orange feels very sad.
Her gift is not
like the other gifts.

Orange tells Strawberry
her gift was just
going to be a hug.

Strawberry thinks a hug
is a perfect gift!

Strawberry says,
"Thank you."
She loves her party
and all her gifts.

But Strawberry loves her berry best friends even more!